THE BOXCAR CHILDREN MYSTERIES

THE BOXCAR CHILDREN
SURPRISE ISLAND
THE YELLOW HOUSE MYSTERY
MYSTERY RANCH
MIKE'S MYSTERY
BLUE BAY MYSTERY
THE WOODSHED MYSTERY
THE LIGHTHOUSE MYSTERY
MOUNTAIN TOP MYSTERY
SCHOOLHOUSE MYSTERY
CABOOSE MYSTERY
HOUSEBOAT MYSTERY
SNOWBOUND MYSTERY
TREE HOUSE MYSTERY
BICYCLE MYSTERY
MYSTERY IN THE SAND
MYSTERY BEHIND THE WALL
BUS STATION MYSTERY
BENNY UNCOVERS A MYSTERY
THE HAUNTED CABIN MYSTERY
THE DESERTED LIBRARY MYSTERY
THE ANIMAL SHELTER MYSTERY
THE OLD MOTEL MYSTERY
THE MYSTERY OF THE HIDDEN PAINTING
THE AMUSEMENT PARK MYSTERY
THE MYSTERY OF THE MIXED-UP ZOO
THE CAMP-OUT MYSTERY
THE MYSTERY GIRL
THE MYSTERY CRUISE
THE DISAPPEARING FRIEND MYSTERY
THE MYSTERY OF THE SINGING GHOST
THE MYSTERY IN THE SNOW
THE PIZZA MYSTERY
THE MYSTERY HORSE
THE MYSTERY AT THE DOG SHOW
THE CASTLE MYSTERY
THE MYSTERY OF THE LOST VILLAGE
THE MYSTERY ON THE ICE
THE MYSTERY OF THE PURPLE POOL
THE GHOST SHIP MYSTERY
THE MYSTERY IN WASHINGTON, DC
THE CANOE TRIP MYSTERY
THE MYSTERY OF THE HIDDEN BEACH
THE MYSTERY OF THE MISSING CAT
THE MYSTERY AT SNOWFLAKE INN
THE MYSTERY ON STAGE
THE DINOSAUR MYSTERY
THE MYSTERY OF THE STOLEN MUSIC
THE MYSTERY AT THE BALL PARK
THE CHOCOLATE SUNDAE MYSTERY
THE MYSTERY OF THE HOT AIR BALLOON
THE MYSTERY BOOKSTORE
THE PILGRIM VILLAGE MYSTERY
THE MYSTERY OF THE STOLEN BOXCAR
THE MYSTERY IN THE CAVE
THE MYSTERY ON THE TRAIN
THE MYSTERY AT THE FAIR
THE MYSTERY OF THE LOST MINE
THE GUIDE DOG MYSTERY
THE HURRICANE MYSTERY
THE PET SHOP MYSTERY
THE MYSTERY OF THE SECRET MESSAGE
THE FIREHOUSE MYSTERY
THE MYSTERY IN SAN FRANCISCO
THE NIAGARA FALLS MYSTERY
THE MYSTERY AT THE ALAMO
THE OUTER SPACE MYSTERY
THE SOCCER MYSTERY
THE MYSTERY IN THE OLD ATTIC
THE GROWLING BEAR MYSTERY
THE MYSTERY OF THE LAKE MONSTER
THE MYSTERY AT PEACOCK HALL
THE WINDY CITY MYSTERY
THE BLACK PEARL MYSTERY
THE CEREAL BOX MYSTERY
THE PANTHER MYSTERY
THE MYSTERY OF THE QUEEN'S JEWELS
THE STOLEN SWORD MYSTERY
THE BASKETBALL MYSTERY
THE MOVIE STAR MYSTERY
THE MYSTERY OF THE PIRATE'S MAP
THE GHOST TOWN MYSTERY
THE MYSTERY OF THE BLACK RAVEN
THE MYSTERY IN THE MALL
THE MYSTERY IN NEW YORK
THE GYMNASTICS MYSTERY
THE POISON FROG MYSTERY
THE MYSTERY OF THE EMPTY SAFE
THE HOME RUN MYSTERY
THE GREAT BICYCLE RACE MYSTERY

THE MYSTERY OF THE WILD PONIES
THE MYSTERY IN THE COMPUTER GAME
THE HONEYBEE MYSTERY
THE MYSTERY AT THE CROOKED HOUSE
THE HOCKEY MYSTERY
THE MYSTERY OF THE MIDNIGHT DOG
THE MYSTERY OF THE SCREECH OWL
THE SUMMER CAMP MYSTERY
THE COPYCAT MYSTERY
THE HAUNTED CLOCK TOWER MYSTERY
THE MYSTERY OF THE TIGER'S EYE
THE DISAPPEARING STAIRCASE MYSTERY
THE MYSTERY ON BLIZZARD MOUNTAIN
THE MYSTERY OF THE SPIDER'S CLUE
THE CANDY FACTORY MYSTERY
THE MYSTERY OF THE MUMMY'S CURSE
THE MYSTERY OF THE STAR RUBY
THE STUFFED BEAR MYSTERY
THE MYSTERY OF ALLIGATOR SWAMP
THE MYSTERY AT SKELETON POINT
THE TATTLETALE MYSTERY
THE COMIC BOOK MYSTERY
THE GREAT SHARK MYSTERY
THE ICE CREAM MYSTERY
THE MIDNIGHT MYSTERY
THE MYSTERY IN THE FORTUNE COOKIE
THE BLACK WIDOW SPIDER MYSTERY
THE RADIO MYSTERY
THE MYSTERY OF THE RUNAWAY GHOST
THE FINDERS KEEPERS MYSTERY
THE MYSTERY OF THE HAUNTED BOXCAR
THE CLUE IN THE CORN MAZE
THE GHOST OF THE CHATTERING BONES
THE SWORD OF THE SILVER KNIGHT
THE GAME STORE MYSTERY
THE MYSTERY OF THE ORPHAN TRAIN
THE VANISHING PASSENGER
THE GIANT YO-YO MYSTERY
THE CREATURE IN OGOPOGO LAKE
THE ROCK 'N' ROLL MYSTERY
THE SECRET OF THE MASK
THE SEATTLE PUZZLE
THE GHOST IN THE FIRST ROW
THE BOX THAT WATCH FOUND
A HORSE NAMED DRAGON
THE GREAT DETECTIVE RACE
THE GHOST AT THE DRIVE-IN MOVIE
THE MYSTERY OF THE TRAVELING TOMATOES
THE SPY GAME
THE DOG-GONE MYSTERY
THE VAMPIRE MYSTERY
SUPERSTAR WATCH
THE SPY IN THE BLEACHERS
THE AMAZING MYSTERY SHOW
THE PUMPKIN HEAD MYSTERY
THE CUPCAKE CAPER
THE CLUE IN THE RECYCLING BIN
MONKEY TROUBLE
THE ZOMBIE PROJECT
THE GREAT TURKEY HEIST
THE GARDEN THIEF
THE BOARDWALK MYSTERY
THE MYSTERY OF THE FALLEN TREASURE
THE RETURN OF THE GRAVEYARD GHOST
THE MYSTERY OF THE STOLEN SNOWBOARD
THE MYSTERY OF THE WILD WEST BANDIT
THE MYSTERY OF THE SOCCER SNITCH
THE MYSTERY OF THE GRINNING GARGOYLE
THE MYSTERY OF THE MISSING POP IDOL
THE MYSTERY OF THE STOLEN DINOSAUR BONES
THE MYSTERY AT THE CALGARY STAMPEDE
THE SLEEPY HOLLOW MYSTERY
THE LEGEND OF THE IRISH CASTLE
THE CELEBRITY CAT CAPER
HIDDEN IN THE HAUNTED SCHOOL
THE ELECTION DAY DILEMMA
JOURNEY ON A RUNAWAY TRAIN
THE CLUE IN THE PAPYRUS SCROLL
THE DETOUR OF THE ELEPHANTS
THE SHACKLETON SABOTAGE
THE KHIPU AND THE FINAL KEY

THE BOXCAR® CHILDREN

BY
GERTRUDE CHANDLER WARNER

MIKE'S MYSTERY

BOOK 5

ILLUSTRATED BY
DIRK GRINGHUIS

ALBERT WHITMAN & COMPANY
CHICAGO, ILLINOIS

ISBN 978-0-8075-5140-0 (hardcover)
ISBN 978-0-8075-5141-7 (paperback)

Printed in the United States of America
104 103 102 101 100 99 LB 22 21 20 19 18 17

Interior illustrations by Dirk Gringhuis

Visit the Boxcar Children online at www.boxcarchildren.com.
For more information about Albert Whitman & Company, visit our website at www.albertwhitman.com.

Contents

CHAPTER		PAGE
1	Yellow Sands	9
2	An Old Friend	15
3	Fire!	27
4	At the Big Table	35
5	The Empty Room	42
6	Mike's Mother's Place	48
7	The Blue Hat	58
8	Secrets	69
9	Quick Work	78
10	Mike's Idea	87
11	Pie Day	97
12	An Empty Can	107
13	The Party	116
14	Ben or Mike?	122

MIKE'S MYSTERY

CHAPTER 1

Yellow Sands

The four Alden children could hardly wait to get back to Mystery Ranch. Henry, Jessie, Violet and Benny had planned for weeks what they would do.

"We'll go on that dear old train!" said Violet. "Remember Mr. Carter who helped us carry our bags, Jessie?"

"I'll carry the bags!" shouted Benny. "Mr. Carter won't be on the train this time."

"Maybe I'll carry some of the bags, old boy," said

Henry. "But you know we won't get off at Centerville."

Jessie nodded at her older brother. "Yes, we will get off at Yellow Sands now. I think that is a beautiful name. Our uranium fields looked just like yellow sand."

Grandfather said, "Sam will meet you. Maybe Sam will carry the bags."

The children laughed. "Fighting over old bags," said Benny.

"Too bad Watch has to ride in the baggage car," said Henry. "But they don't allow dogs anywhere else on the train."

"I'll ride in the baggage car, too," said Benny. "Then he won't mind."

Mr. Alden laughed. He said, "I'm afraid you can't do that. But you can go and see him once in a while. Then he will know you are near by."

At last the day came when they were off to Mystery Ranch where Aunt Jane lived.

Henry, Jessie, Violet and Benny loved Aunt Jane

and they were to visit her for the summer vacation.

Once she had been a very cross old woman. But now she was a very pleasant lady.

When they got off the train at Yellow Sands, they all looked for the old black horse. But instead they saw Sam and Maggie with a station wagon. Sam took care of the ranch, and Maggie took care of Aunt Jane.

"Hello, Sam!" cried Benny. "Where's Snowball?"

"Snowball's all right," said Sam smiling. "I always thought that was a funny name for a black horse."

"I named him," said Benny. "I thought it was a funny name, too. Where is he?"

"He is taking it easy these days," said Maggie. "He stays out in the field all the time eating grass. This car goes faster."

"You mean you can drive it, Maggie?" asked Jessie.

"Yes," said Maggie smiling. "Sam says I drive all right."

"Let's go," said Sam. "Now that Watch is out of the baggage car, we are ready."

Everyone carried a bag. In no time they were going

through the new gate to Aunt Jane's house. At the top of the gate were big letters saying, *Mystery Ranch.*

How glad Aunt Jane was to see them! Watch did not care much for Aunt Jane's new dog, Lady. But when lunch was ready, Watch lay down at Jessie's foot, and Lady lay down at Aunt Jane's foot. So all was well.

"Oh, this place has changed in just this one year," Aunt Jane said. "You would never know it. There is one long street down the middle of my old hay field."

"Is it a real street?" asked Benny.

"Oh, my, yes! There are lots of stores and a church, and a school and a High School."

"I can't imagine it," said Henry. "We shall have to go and see it soon."

"Go any time you like," said Aunt Jane. "I know you are just dying to see that street."

"We want to see you, too, Aunt Jane," said Violet.

"Well, you've seen me now," said Aunt Jane.

MYSTERY RANCH

"Lunch is over. So you go along and enjoy yourselves."

"Be back for supper," said Maggie. "We are going to have a fine supper."

"Oh, we will get back long before supper," said Jessie. "We just want to see what the old ranch looks like."

CHAPTER 2

An Old Friend

The ranch belonged to the four Alden children. So, of course, they wanted to see how it had changed since last summer when uranium had been found.

Benny said, "I suppose Grandfather had to get hundreds of miners to work in the uranium mine. And the miners have lots of children, and they must have clothes and something to eat, and a school and a church. So that's how the town grew."

"Right!" said Henry with a smile. "You have it all worked out." The four children went out the back door.

"Yes, Watch, you can come," said Henry to the dog. "Can Lady come too, Aunt Jane?"

"No," said Aunt Jane. "Lady always stays with me."

Watch was delighted to go with the four children, so he barked and barked. He ran along barking. On they went, past the hen houses. These were all mended and painted. They went through a field to the street. It was very strange to see a city street in the middle of the old field.

"There's a five and ten," said Benny, "and a big super-market! We won't need to hoe any vegetables if we don't want to."

"What a beautiful dress shop!" said Jessie. Then she almost bumped into a boy about Benny's age. He was walking with his hands in his pockets and he was whistling.

When he saw the children he stopped and stared at them. Then he said, "Hi, Ben! Don't you know me?"

Benny took one look. "Mike! Mike Wood!" he

yelled. "It's Mike, Henry! Remember he came to the picnic on Surprise Island?"

"Well, I'd never forget that," said Henry. "It is Mike, sure enough! You came over to our picnic and your dog had a race with Watch."

"Yep," said Mike. "That was my dog Spotty. He's out with my brother Pat now. I remember how he beat your dog in the race."

"Oh, *no!*" cried Benny. "He never did! Watch was the one that beat Spotty! Don't you remember?"

"No, I don't," said Mike. "I know Spot beat Watch."

"He didn't either!" shouted Benny. "Spot was a stranger. He didn't even know which way to run!"

"Stop, you boys," cried Henry. "Don't fight the minute you meet."

"Well, Mike started it," shouted Benny.

"I did not! You started it," shouted Mike.

"Boys!" said Henry. "Stop this minute. Aren't you friends?"

"We're friends," said Benny, "unless Mike tells lies

about Watch. Watch won that race and I won't give in for anybody."

"Well," said Mike, "maybe he did. But it wasn't a fair race, because Spotty didn't even know the way."

"O.K." said Benny. "That's all I care. If you say Spotty didn't beat."

"Well, maybe he didn't beat," said Mike, "but how could he beat when he didn't know where to run?"

"Well, he couldn't," said Benny. "That's what I said. He couldn't and he didn't. I never said it was a fair race."

"Mike," said Jessie pleasantly, "how did you happen to come out here? You're so far from where we saw you last."

"I know," said Mike. "But we like it here. My Uncle Bob invited us to live here when my father died. Uncle Bob said he could give Pat a job. Remember Pat? My big brother?"

"Oh, yes," said Henry. "He was the one who almost got drowned at the picnic."

"Well, Pat works at the mine for my Uncle Bob.

Not in the mine, but outside. I do all sorts of work for the mine, too. We all work. Mother washes the miners' clothes."

"Where's your house?" asked Henry.

"Over there," said Mike, pointing. "That pink one. The houses are all alike, only different colors. Each house has a yard around it, but the grass is dry and brown. My house has an electric stove and a washing machine. It's different from our old house back home. Come and see my mother."

"All right," said Henry. "We'd like to."

"Pat isn't home, but my mother is," said Mike. "She is making a pie, maybe, and we could have some to eat."

They reached the door of the pink house. "Ma, look who's here!" said Mike.

Mrs. Wood was indeed making pies. She was taking the third pie out of the oven. When she looked up and saw Benny, she laughed out loud.

"Hello, Benny Alden!" she cried.

"You have never seen the rest of us," said Jessie,

laughing. "But you have seen plenty of Benny, when he went to school with Mike back in the East."

"I've heard lots about you," said Mrs. Wood. "Benny is a great talker. He's a fine boy. It does Mike good to play with him."

"It does Ben good to play with me," said Mike loudly.

"Yes, I think it does," agreed Henry.

Mike looked up in surprise. He did not know what to say. He thought Henry would not agree with him. "Ma makes pies for the neighbors," he said.

"And you are surely neighbors," said Mrs. Wood at once. "So take your choice. I have cherry, apple, and blueberry pie. All hot." She began cutting the three pies. The smell was delicious and the pie crusts were brown and flaky.

"I didn't really have much lunch," said Benny.

"Pull up your chairs around that table," said Mrs. Wood. "And Mike, you get a bit of cheese out of the refrigerator."

"Where's Pat?" asked Mike, getting the cheese.

"Gone to the bank. It's pay day. He puts Uncle Bob's money in the bank every week. You go get him, Mike, and tell him to come home and see the company."

Mike ran off down the street. Mrs. Wood watched him with a smile.

"He's not a bad boy, is Mike," she said. "He's just a big talker."

"We know that," said Jessie, smiling too.

"He'd do anything for his friends," said his mother. "He helps the men at the mine a lot, even if he fights, too. They joke with him and argue with him, but they like him."

Henry said, "This is the best apple pie I ever ate."

"I agree," said Jessie. "The cherry must be even better than the apple."

Violet laughed softly. "I was going to say the same thing about this blueberry."

"I'm glad," said Mrs. Wood very quietly. "I love to bake pies the best of anything. I wish I had time."

"Haven't you time?" asked Jessie, puzzled.

"No, dear," said Mrs. Wood. Her voice sounded sad. "I wash all day to earn money to help keep us. I'm lucky to have a washing machine. Here's Pat now."

When Pat came in, he said at once, "Hello, Ben! You used to come down to our house and play with Mike."

"This is Jessie," said his mother. "This is Violet, and this is Henry."

"Oh, I know them all," said Pat. "They saved my life on that picnic."

"Our cousin Joe did that," said Henry. "He is a fine swimmer."

Then Mike said, "When I met Pat, he was just coming out of the bank."

"It seems too funny to have a bank here," said Jessie. "This whole place used to be great fields of long grass."

"We have almost everything," said Pat. "We have a newspaper every day. The newspaper office is right by the bank."

"Oh, yes," cried Benny. "I saw the paper up at Aunt Jane's. The Daily News. It had a big picture of the uranium mine buildings on the front page."

"Yes, the mine is almost always on the front page," said Mike. "Here it is. We saved this one, because Pat is in the picture. See, right there? That's Pat. Standing by the short man. Gosh, that's funny. I've seen that man before some place. He don't live here."

"Doesn't," said Pat.

"Well, doesn't, then," said Mike. "You say *Don't* to me often enough."

"That's very different, Mike," said Pat.

"Well, it don't sound any different to me," said Mike.

Jessie laughed. "Mike makes me think of Benny, sometimes," she said. "They both love to argue."

"I'm not arguing," said Mike. "I'm thinking. That short man in the picture don't—doesn't—live around here. He's a stranger. But I know I've seen him before."

Pat looked at the picture. "I don't remember him

at all," he said to his younger brother. "I didn't even know when they took the picture."

Mike was very quiet for a while. He kept looking at the picture.

"We must go," said Jessie. "We want to go into every store on the street and see all the sights."

"I'll go with you," said Mike. "I can show you everything. I've been here two months."

It was true. Mike did know everything. He

showed them the door of the super-market which opened all by itself. He showed them a garage where new cars were for sale. Jessie bought five big straw hats in one store. The sun was very hot, so they all put on the hats. Everyone in the stores seemed to know who the children were. Aunt Jane had put their pictures in the paper many times since they owned the ranch where uranium had been found.

At last Jessie said, "Come on, let's go home. Maggie said she had a fine supper."

"Thank you, Mike, for showing us," said Violet.

"See you tomorrow, Mike," said Benny.

"Yep," said Mike. He went off whistling. He didn't know then that tomorrow would be so exciting.

CHAPTER 3

Fire!

The children slept soundly. They all woke up once to hear a loud, strange bell ringing. But they thought it was midnight, so they all went to sleep again. When they came down in the morning, Sam and Maggie were talking about a fire.

"What fire?" asked Henry.

"Didn't you hear the firebells ringing and ringing in the night?" asked Sam. "Here comes the paper boy. The news will be in the paper."

Sam took the paper. It was full of pictures. Benny

looked over his shoulder. "It's Mike's house!" yelled Benny at the top of his voice.

"The paper says that it was the Wood's house that had burned to the ground."

"Let me see the paper, Benny," Jessie cried. "I can read faster."

"I can read fast enough," said Benny excitedly. "See that picture? It's Mike all right."

"I'm afraid it is," said Jessie, trying to read. "That lovely new, pink house, and the washing machine and electric stove!"

"No lives were lost," read Benny. "Not even the dog. Their big dog, Spotty, who slept in the cellar barked and gave the alarm. The fire had started in the cellar, and by the time the fire engine came, the whole house was burning. The fire seemed to start on all four sides of the house.

"Nothing was saved except clothing and bedding. When Mrs. Wood saw that the house could not be saved, she put some sheets on the floor, threw all the clothes from bureau drawers and closets on the sheets, tied them up, and threw them out of the window."

"Well, wasn't that smart?" said Jessie. "That costs the most of anything, doesn't it, Aunt Jane? The family clothes and bedding?"

"Yes, my dear," replied her aunt. "I wonder what the Wood family will do now."

"I have to go right down there," said Benny. "I have to see Mike."

"Wait a minute, Benny," said Aunt Jane. "You must eat your breakfast, first. When you get down there, you won't come back for a long time. I know you!"

Benny knew that this was true, so he sat down and tried to eat. They all tried to eat, but everyone was thinking about the fire.

"Mike could come here for a few days," said Aunt Jane, "if he has no other place to go."

"Oh, Aunt Jane, thank you!" said Jessie. "You are very kind. But I don't think you want Mike. He would upset everything."

"I don't mind being upset," said Aunt Jane. "Benny

and Mike would be something amusing to watch."

"You can say that again!" said Henry, laughing.

"I ate an egg," said Benny. "Can I go now?"

"Yes, go along. I know you can hardly wait to get down to the fire," said Aunt Jane.

The children ran all the way. They soon saw a big crowd of people who had come to see the fire. The little pink house was gone. Smoke was still rising from the burned wood, and it was still very hot.

"Hi, Ben!" called a voice. It was Mike. He came running over to Benny. He cried, "That was our house that burned, Ben. We all got out, and it was Spotty saved us."

"What are you going to do, Mike?" asked Henry. "Where is your mother?"

"She's right over there," said Mike pointing. "She and my brother Pat can sleep next door in the blue house, but I am going to stay with Mr. Carter."

"Mr. *Carter!*" cried Jessie. "What Mr. Carter? Do you mean Mr. John Carter?"

"I guess so," said Mike. "That's his name anyway.

Do you know him? He's nice and very friendly."

"He works for Grandfather," said Jessie. "We met him last summer, but we didn't know he was still here. Where does he live?"

"In the green house right near the mine. He has lots of rooms he don't use."

"*Doesn't*," said Benny.

"Now don't you go teaching me, Ben!" said Mike.

"Where is Mr. Carter, now?" asked Violet just in time to stop a fight.

"Right over beside my mother," said Mike. "Come on, they are looking at us."

"Well, well, Mr. Carter!" cried Henry. "We are so glad to see you again. You always seem to pop up when there is trouble."

"I try to," said John Carter with a twinkle in his eye. "Hello, Jessie! And Violet. Benny is still his same old self."

"What will happen to Mike's family?" asked Henry.

"All these houses belong to the Uranium Company. So when the place cools off, the pink house will be built again," replied the man.

"How about the things inside? The washing machine?" asked Jessie.

"I don't know, but insurance will take care of some things later."

"Aunt Jane said Mike could come up to our house," said Violet.

"Oh, did she indeed!" said Mr. Carter, laughing. "You'll have a lively time! Don't you want me, too?"

"You would be a big help," said Jessie, smiling.

"You can have a whole room, Mike, if you come to Aunt Jane's," said Benny. "You'd better ask your mother if you can come."

"Yes, I'm willing, and thankful, too," said Mrs. Wood. "But tell Miss Alden to send Mike back if he gets too much for her."

Then Benny asked suddenly, "Mike! Have you had anything to eat?"

"No!" shouted Mike. "It all burned up. I didn't have any milk, or any oatmeal, or any eggs—"

"Come on, Mike!" shouted Benny. "I could eat another egg myself. Let's all go to the restaurant!"

Mr. Carter looked at Jessie and laughed. He said, "I wonder what's the matter with me? I never even thought of breakfast! And Mrs. Wood, you must be starved. We'll all go to the restaurant and have breakfast."

"We follow Benny as usual," said Mrs. Wood smiling. "He has the ideas."

CHAPTER 4

At the Big Table

Let's all sit at the big table," said Henry. "Then we can talk."

"I don't want to talk. I want to eat!" shouted Mike.

"Then you can keep still all you want," said Benny. "We'll do the talking."

"But I'll say something if I want to," argued Mike.

"Well, make up your mind," returned Benny. "You're the one that said you didn't want to talk."

"I only said I was hungry," said Mike.

"Oh, stop it, Mike," said his mother. "All this talk

about nothing. Don't you know you have no home?"

"That sounds awful," said Jessie. "Tell me, how did you know the house was on fire?"

"The dog," said Mrs. Wood. "Spotty was down in the cellar. He sleeps down there. He barked and barked. I knew something was wrong, so I went down to see. There was fire on all four sides. I let the dog out and woke up Mike and Pat."

"You didn't wake me," said Mike. "I was awake."

"Yes, you were, son," agreed his mother. "I will say you were going down to get the dog yourself."

"Spotty was the most important one," said Mike, "because he can't open doors."

"By the way, where is the dog?" asked Mr. Carter.

"He's tied up at the blue house," said Pat. "He was in the way, barking at everyone."

"Yes, we had to leave Watch and Lady at the ranch, too," said Jessie. "A fire is no place for dogs."

"It is very queer that the fire started in four places at once," said Mr. Carter.

"I wonder if anyone set the fire," said Henry.

"Oh, no!" cried Mrs. Wood. "Why would anybody set fire to our house?"

"What do you plan to do now, Mrs. Wood?" asked Mr. Carter.

"I really don't know," she answered. "I'm staying in the blue house with my good neighbor, Mrs. Smith, for tonight."

Breakfast came then. The eight hungry people went to work on the bacon and eggs, toast, and cereal and milk. For a minute the restaurant was very still. Then the children heard a man say, "I heard that the boy who lived there set the house on fire just for fun."

In an instant Mike was out of his chair. He ran over and faced the man who had spoken. "I did not!" he shouted. "Who says I did?"

In another minute all four children were behind Mike.

"Mike never did!" shouted Benny. "He wouldn't! Who says he did?"

The man laughed a little. He was very much surprised. "Well, don't get so excited, sonny," he said.

"Don't get excited?" yelled Mike. "You told a lie about me!"

"I didn't say it," said the man. "I said I heard it."

Then Henry spoke. "Can you tell us who told you? You must know this story is very bad for Mike."

"Well, well," said the man. "You're not afraid to stand up for a friend, are you?"

"No, sir," said Henry.

Jessie said, "Mike likes fun, yes. He gets into trouble. But he would never set his own house on fire."

Then Benny went right up to the man. He said, "Mike wouldn't set a fire in the cellar anyway. His dog was there."

"So his dog was there," repeated the man. "That settles it. I believe you."

"Who told you?" asked Mike. He was not yelling now.

"I don't know him," said the man. "He was a stranger to me. He stood beside me in the crowd,

watching the fire. I think that he wore a blue hat."

"I'll ask him," said Benny, "if I ever see a man with a blue hat."

The man looked at the four of them. "I wish I had as many good friends as you have, Mike," he said. He looked at Benny. "This one here is a wonderful friend."

"He don't always stand up for me," said Mike.

"Doesn't," said Benny.

"Now look here, Ben!" said Mike. "Don't start that again!"

"You see how Mike is," said Jessie. "He will fight over nothing. But he would never set a fire. Come on back, boys, and eat your breakfast."

The children moved away. All this time Mr. Carter had sat still watching. "Well, Jessie!" he said. "That was just like a play! I am very proud of all of you."

"Why didn't you come over, too?" asked Benny.

"You didn't need me," said Mr. Carter laughing. "You children did it much better than I would. But the man could see I was with you if you needed help."

Mike began to eat again.

"That gave me a good appetite," he said.

"Your appetite was all right before," said Henry, laughing.

"I like to have you with us, Mike," said Violet, laughing. "Now if you weren't here, I couldn't eat my breakfast at all."

"That's right," said Henry. "She couldn't."

"Now everyone watch out for a man with a blue hat," said Benny drinking the last of his milk.

"That man would change his hat, Ben," said Mike. "Maybe he will have a black hat next time. Maybe no hat at all."

"I'll watch, too," said Mr. Carter. "You can be sure of that."

CHAPTER 5

The Empty Room

I have to go up to the uranium mine," said Mr. Carter. "You can all come with me if you want."

"I think I'll go to my neighbor's," said Mrs. Wood. "I'm all tired out with Mike's doings."

"Yes, I'll go with you, Ma," said Pat. "Maybe I can help around the place, to pay for taking us in."

"The rest of us will go with you, Mr. Carter," said Benny. "It's our own mine after all, and we haven't seen it yet. You come too, Mike."

"Well, Benny, you are asking for trouble," said Henry laughing.

"I'm no *trouble*," cried Mike. "I might help you. I know a lot of things."

Soon they were on their way to the mine in Mr. Carter's car. When they arrived, they could see great machines at work. Workmen were everywhere. Mr. Carter stopped his car at a large building. It had a small office in one corner.

"I'm going into the office for a few minutes," said Mr. Carter. "You may stay in the car and watch the men. But you must not go any closer than you are now."

"Can't we go into the big building?" asked Benny.

Mr. Carter said, "Oh, yes, you can do that. But it is empty. Just one big room. Nothing to see. I'll be back soon."

When Mr. Carter had shut the office door, Mike said, "I bet he's going to find out about insurance on our things and tell someone in there about the blue hat."

"Yes," said Benny. "Let's see what is in that empty room."

Benny got out of the car and quietly walked into the big, empty room. Jessie followed him. They stood looking around.

"A big room going to waste, Jessie!" said Benny.

"Yes, Benny," said his sister. For a minute they said nothing more. Jessie was thinking about what Benny had said—a big room going to waste.

"Look, Benny!" she said excitedly. "Do you remember what Mrs. Wood said about baking?"

"Yes, I do. She said she loved to bake pies and she didn't like to wash."

"That's just right, Benny! Now listen! If we could get a good stove—"

"Mrs. Wood could bake in it," finished Benny.

"And right here in this very room," said Henry. One by one the others had come inside, too.

Then another gentle voice said, "I'm sure Grandfather would let us buy a stove." It was Violet. She was smiling.

"My mother likes to make pies the best," said Mike. "On pies she is a wizard."

Henry laughed. "Well, now that we are all here, let's get together on this."

"My mother could sell pies to the miners," said Mike. "There's about a million men, I should say. We could make money. And I could eat pies whenever I wanted to," Mike finished.

"If we had a stove," said Benny.

"Not quite a million men," said Henry. "Maybe a hundred or more."

"Maybe we could all live up here," said Mike.

"You wouldn't want to live here, Mike," said Benny. "Wait till you see your room at Aunt Jane's. Right next to me."

"We'll ask Mr. Carter what he thinks," said Jessie. "He knows everything and he will settle it."

But it was really Mrs. Wood who settled it.

CHAPTER 6

Mike's Mother's Place

Benny began to talk the minute he got into the car. Mike began to talk too.

"Wait, boys," said Mr. Carter. "One at a time! I can't hear a word you say."

"I'll talk first," said Mike.

"Well, you can this time," agreed Benny. "It's about your own mother, after all."

"That's right, Ben," said Mike. "Thank you. Mr. Carter, my mother works hard at her washing, but she don't—doesn't like it."

"Yes, Mike," said Mr. Carter. "But what do you want me to do about it?"

"We've thought of a good job for her," said Mike. "She loves to make pies. So why not make pies and sell them? She gives away millions of pies."

"Now, Mike," said Benny. "Mr. Carter won't believe you, if you say millions."

"Well, dozens, then," said Mike.

"Good for you, Mike," said Mr. Carter laughing. "I do believe you, for I have eaten many of those pies myself."

"Well, there you are," said Mike. "Everyone likes Ma's pies and everyone will buy them."

Then Mr. Carter said, "I think you are wasting time telling me about this plan. Why don't we go ask your mother? She is the one to decide."

Mrs. Wood was surprised when they all came back to Mrs. Smith's blue house.

Henry said, "Hello, Mrs. Wood. We want you to come up to the office at the uranium mine for a few minutes."

"All right," said Mrs. Wood. "I'd like to go. I know the night watchman up there, and I'd like to take him a cherry pie."

"You mean you've made another pie already?" asked Violet.

"I made four more," said Mrs. Wood. "They are for the kind people who helped me get out of my burning house. One is for your Aunt Jane, Benny. My neighbor gave me the shortening and filling for the pies, and I will pay her back in washing."

Mike winked at Benny. "Maybe, yes," he said. "And maybe, no."

The children talked and laughed all the way to the mine. They could hardly wait to show the room to Mike's mother. At last they all stood in the big empty room.

"See this room going to waste!" cried Benny. "Now if you had a nice stove—"

Mrs. Wood put her arm around Benny. "What a kind little boy you are, Benny!" she said in a low voice. "I begin to see now what you are all planning for me."

"You mean you like the idea of making pies for a living?" asked Jessie. "Wouldn't you get tired of making pies?"

"I'd never be tired of making pies, my dear!" cried Mrs. Wood. "I love to mix them up, and roll them out, and fill them with cherries, apples, peaches, or blueberries. And best of all I like to see people eat them."

A man behind them said, "I'd rather eat them than watch other people eat them." Everyone turned around.

"The night watchman!" cried Mike. "Hello, Mr. McCarthy!"

"Hello yourself, Mike," said the man.

"Oh, Mr. McCarthy," said Mrs. Wood. "Here's a cherry pie I made for you. I hope you will like it." She gave him the cherry pie.

"Is there anyone in the whole world that doesn't like your pies?" asked Mr. McCarthy. He looked at the children. "What's this I hear about selling pies?"

Mike began to jump around. "See this room!" he

shouted. "Ma can have a stove in that corner. She can bake her pies in it. She can sell them at that big window and we will all help her."

"Well, well," cried Mr. McCarthy. "And which of you thought of this?"

"My sister Jessie was the first to think of it," said Benny. "But I was next to the first, wasn't I, Henry?"

"Yes, you were," said Henry. "We have to buy a sink and a refrigerator, Mr. McCarthy. And we have to ask Mr. Gardner, the boss, for the use of the room."

"We can ask Grandfather to let us buy the sink and things," said Violet.

"Suppose this grandfather of yours won't let you buy all that?" said Mr. McCarthy. "After all, it will cost a lot of money. Not many men would trust children with this plan."

"My grandfather will," said Benny. "We were all alone in the Boxcar. We didn't know Grandfather then. And we did all right."

Mr. Carter nodded at the night watchman. He

said, "Mr. Alden trusts these children. He always tries to help them with their ideas."

The night watchman looked at Jessie with a funny little smile. "I can't understand why you children want to work at all. Don't you own the mine? Your grandfather ought not to let you work."

Jessie shook her head. She said, "That's not the way Grandfather thinks. He has lots of money already. But he says everyone ought to work. Nobody can be happy unless he has some work to do. We know he is right, for we were very, very happy when we didn't have any money at all. Only $4! When we get through school, Grandfather wants us all to go to work for a living."

"There are not many grandfathers like that," said Mr. McCarthy, shaking his head. "And I know well that Mr. Alden works very hard himself."

"What do you think of this pie business, Mr. McCarthy?" asked Jessie.

"I? Hm-m, I think the men will want so many pies, that one woman can't make enough."

"Maybe you'll tell the men about the pies?" said Henry.

"Tell them? I won't need to. The minute they see a sign here saying PIES they will all come over."

"Sign?" cried Benny. "Did you say a sign? I'll tell you a good sign. *Mike's Mother's Place!*"

"Oh, I'll paint the sign!" cried Violet.

"Wonderful!" said Jessie. "And what a wonderful name for this place!"

Mrs. Wood smiled and smiled, but she had tears in

her eyes. "Yes," she said, "the men all know Mike, and they will soon know his mother."

"We can take pictures of this place when it is all set to go," said Henry. "They will put them in the paper, maybe."

Mr. McCarthy went over to the big window. "Yes," he said, "this big window will be good for selling pies."

Mike went over to Mr. McCarthy. He said softly, "Did you see my fire?"

"No," said the watchman, "I missed it."

"It was a terrible fire," said Mike. "Everybody went to see it. Why didn't you go? Aren't you interested in fires?"

Mr. McCarthy looked at Mike. He said, "Well, son, I was certainly interested. In fact I started to go. But you see my duty was here. I'm a watchman."

"Too bad," said Mike. "It was a sight."

"I know," said Mr. McCarthy. "But I thought I saw somebody near the mine. So I stayed right here. I looked all around but I couldn't find anybody."

"Come on, Mike!" called Benny. "What are you talking about?"

Then Mike surprised everyone. He began to jump up and down and yell, "The blue hat! The blue hat!"

"What in the world is the matter with you, Mike?" asked Henry.

Mike answered, "I think I know how to find out who wore the blue hat," he yelled.

Mr. Carter stared at the little boy. "Do you indeed!" he said. "You ought to join the FBI."

CHAPTER 7

The Blue Hat

All the children begged Mike to tell what he knew about the man in the blue hat.

"No," said Mike. "I can't tell you now. I want to talk to Ben about this. I want to see Ben alone."

"This is very important, Mike," said Mr. Carter. "If you know something it is your duty to tell me."

"Oh, I'll tell you all right," said Mike. "Only you'll have to wait about one hour."

"Why all the mystery?" asked Mr. Carter.

"Because I'm not sure," said Mike. "I'm not really sure of anything. I want to see Pat, too."

"Well, let's go back to the ranch," said Henry. He did not think Mike really knew anything about the stranger.

"We have hardly seen Aunt Jane," said Violet. "We have been away almost all the time we have been here."

"That was because there was a fire," said Benny. "We had to see about Mike's fire."

Mr. Carter took the five children to Aunt Jane's house. Then he drove away. He said he had other business. Watch and Lady ran out to meet the children. The dogs were very glad to see them.

"Well," said Maggie, "you are not late. But I thought you were going to be. And we have a very funny lunch."

"What is it?" asked Benny.

"Hot dogs," said Maggie. "Your Aunt Jane says all young people like hot dogs."

"We do!" cried Benny. "And we don't get them very often. Hurrah for Aunt Jane!"

"Tell me all the news about the fire," said Aunt

Jane. She sat at the head of the table. She gave the hot dogs to the children, but she did not eat them herself.

"I don't like hot dogs," she said smiling. "I like eggs better."

The children took turns with the news. They told Aunt Jane all about the fire and meeting Mr. Carter again. They told her the plans for Mrs. Wood. Mike was very quiet. He did not talk very much.

"Mike is scared of you, Aunt Jane!" said Benny.

"I am not scared!" said Mike. "Miss Alden wouldn't hurt a fly. My brother Pat said so."

"I certainly wouldn't hurt a nice boy like you, Mike," said Aunt Jane laughing. "You must go up and see your new room. It is right next to Benny's."

Maggie said, "We have been working on it all morning. A nice clean bed, and a big empty closet for your things."

"I haven't many things," said Mike.

"Haven't you any old birds' nests and stones and model airplanes?" asked Maggie.

"Oh, can I keep that kind of things?" cried Mike.

"Certainly," said Aunt Jane. "There's no good living here, if you can't have your own things."

"Oh, oh!" cried Mike. "Can I have Spotty, too?"

"Yes," said Aunt Jane. "Lady always stays in my room." She stopped. "But what will Watch say?"

"I don't think he will say much," said Mike. "They didn't fight on Surprise Island."

"That's right," said Henry to Aunt Jane. "They got along all right."

"I'll be fine if I have Spotty," said Mike.

"He mustn't get up on your nice clean bed," said Maggie.

"Oh, no, he sleeps down the cellar when he's home," said Mike.

Aunt Jane said, "He won't sleep down the cellar here. You can have him in your room, but Maggie says not on your bed."

Then Mike was quiet again. He seemed to be thinking.

After lunch, Henry telephoned to his grandfather

miles away in Greenfield. He told Mr. Alden all about the fire. He didn't know that his grandfather knew it already. Mr. Carter had already called Mr. Alden.

"You say you know this boy Mike?" asked Mr. Alden.

"Yes, he used to go to school with Benny. We invited him to the picnic on Surprise Island."

"Oh, I remember," said Mr. Alden. "He had a brother who was almost drowned."

"Good for you, Grandfather!" cried Henry. "You never forget anything. Mike's mother hasn't any home now, and we want to give her that big empty room at the mine to make pies in."

Mr. Alden said, "Is that all you want, Henry?"

"Almost," said Henry. "We'd like to buy a stove, and a sink, and a refrigerator for the room. We can buy them all here."

"Go ahead, Henry," said Mr. Alden. "It's your money and your mine. It's a fine idea and a kind one. I had a plan for that room, but it can wait. This is more important. If you need anything more, ask Mr. Carter. And how is Watch?"

"Watch is right here, looking at me," said Henry. "You speak to him, Grandfather."

"Hello, Watch!" called Mr. Alden.

"Bow-wow!" answered the dog. He put his feet up on the telephone table and wagged his tail.

"I heard him bark," said Mr. Alden, laughing. "And now I'll talk to the others." Mr. Alden always did this. He talked with Violet, and Jessie and Aunt Jane and Benny.

"I'm the last one, Grandfather," said Benny. "But I was the next to the first to think of the stove."

"I'm sure you were, Benny," said his grandfather. "You be a good boy, and take good care of the girls."

"Yes, I will," said Benny. "You know what? They want a blue refrigerator! I want a white one, but I'll give in."

"Good boy," said Mr. Alden. "Good-by for now."

After the telephone call, Mike said he wanted to see Benny alone.

"Come up and see your room," said Benny. "Then we can talk."

Mike had no idea what a lovely room he would have. He looked around in surprise.

"This is neat, Ben," he said. "And right next to you."

"My wall paper has jet planes on it," said Benny. "Aunt Jane picked it out for me. She's neat, too."

"Listen, Ben," said Mike. "When we were up at the mine, I remembered something."

"What was it?" asked Benny. The two boys sat down on the floor. They put their heads together.

"Well, you know I said we had to tie Spotty up because he barked?"

"I remember," said Benny.

"Well, he did bark. He barked at everyone, and he barked at the fire. He was so excited. But once he growled, Ben."

"Oh, ho! I see!" cried Benny. "That's different. What did he growl at?"

"The man in the blue hat!" cried Mike. "I really

don't remember what hat he had on. But I think I saw him at the fire. He was the one Spotty growled at."

"I suppose Spotty never growls," said Benny.

"Never!" said Mike. "Unless he has some good reason. Now another thing, Ben. You remember the newspaper picture of Pat? Now, I ought to have been in that picture."

"Why?" asked Benny.

"Well, I was right beside Pat. The picture cut me off. I was always up at the mine before you came. I knew everybody. And I saw that stranger myself. He was a short man."

Benny nodded. "Did you talk to him?"

"No, I didn't. But I saw him talking to Mr. McCarthy. And I think he was the man Spotty growled at!"

"Oh, you do!" cried Benny. "Then he must be the man that said you set the fire!"

"That's right," said Mike. "Isn't that a mystery?"

"Yes, it is," agreed Benny. "The next thing to do is see Mr. McCarthy."

"Right!" said Mike. "But we won't rush it! Mr.

Carter said I ought to become an FBI agent."

"Yes, he did," said Benny. "And I'd like to see that newspaper picture again."

So the two boys ran downstairs to find the old newspaper.

CHAPTER 8

Secrets

Everyone looked for the newspaper, but no one could find it.

"All the newspapers are in that box," said Maggie. "I saved them all."

"They are all here but the right one," said Benny.

"I had one, but it burned up with my house," said Mike.

"Well, never mind," said Aunt Jane. "You can always buy another at the newspaper office."

Henry said, "Mike, you know this is the time we

buy a stove. You can look at the newspaper any time."

"This is a very important paper," said Benny. "But I guess we can wait."

"Well, come on then," said Jessie. "What fun it will be to get all those things! I never bought a stove before."

"Don't you think Mrs. Wood ought to go with us?" asked Violet. "She ought to pick out the stove she wants."

"Right, as usual," said Henry. "Come on, let's go. Yes, Watch, you can come this time." Lady stayed with Aunt Jane, as she always did.

The children stopped at the blue house. Mrs. Wood was glad to go with them.

"Let's take Spotty, too," said Mike.

"He doesn't like to be tied up. He'd love to go."

"Will he like to go with Watch?" asked Jessie.

"Let's try," said Mike. Everyone was glad when at last the two dogs trotted along together.

The store was a big one. There were all sorts of things in it. There were tables and chairs and stoves and dishes of all kinds. Mrs. Wood looked around. She was delighted to pick out a huge stove. It had large ovens. The refrigerator was big too.

"It will have to be big for all those pies," said Benny. "What color do you want, Mrs. Wood?"

"Well, I don't care at all," said Mike's mother.

"The girls like blue," said Benny.

"Let's get all blue things, then," said Mrs. Wood. "Just look at that beautiful blue sink!"

The man said, "We will put them all in for you. Where do they go?"

"In that big empty building at the mine office," said Henry. "My grandfather said to pay you when they were all in."

"That's O.K.," said the man with a smile.

"Mr. Carter says insurance will pay for our loss from the fire," said Mrs. Wood. "I hope so, because we lost almost everything."

"Oh, Mrs. Wood, let's buy dishes!" cried Violet.

Everyone looked at Violet in surprise. Violet was usually so quiet.

SOLD
SOLD
SOLD

SOLD

Jessie put her arm around her sister. "You dear," she said. "We will certainly buy dishes. Is that all right with you, Mrs. Wood?"

"Yes, I love to have you help me," said Mrs. Wood. "You have such good ideas."

"Where will you put the dishes?" asked the storekeeper. "You're not going to live up at the mine, are you?"

"Live there? Oh, no," said Mrs. Wood. "But we can put the dishes up there for now."

"Why *couldn't* you live there?" asked Benny, suddenly. "You've got to live *somewhere*."

"And it will take a long time to build the pink house again," added Henry.

"Yes, I don't like to stay too long with Mrs. Smith," said Mrs. Wood. "I shall have to live somewhere. I wonder if there is anyone at the mine all night?"

"There are four watchmen," said Henry. "I found that out. Then Mr. Carter lives in the green house. That's the nearest house."

"I shall talk with Mr. Carter," said Mrs. Wood.

"But we must pick out the bowls and dishes, first."

"What lovely colors!" said Jessie.

There were plates and cups of all colors, pink, blue, yellow, green, violet and light orange.

"Why don't you have one plate of each color?" asked Benny. "That would make six."

"I must have seven," said Mrs. Wood with a laugh. "Because you must all come to supper sometime."

Jessie said firmly, "I think you need a dozen, Mrs. Wood. That would be two of each color."

"Yes," said Benny. "And then I could use the pink cup—I mean if I ever came to supper."

Jessie laughed. "Benny has a pink cup at home," she told Mrs. Wood. "He loves it because he had it in the Boxcar. I certainly would not like to break that pink cup."

"We must have knives and forks, spoons, and pans, too," said Mrs. Wood.

The storekeeper seemed to be thinking. At last he said, "Mrs. Wood, may I say something? I wouldn't buy too many things if I were you."

"Why on earth not?" cried Mike.

"Well, I can't say too much," said the man. "But I know your friends are going to give you some things."

"Oh, how kind they are!" cried Mrs. Wood. "I never thought of such a thing!"

"Don't tell I told you," said the man.

"We won't tell, any of us," said Benny. "It would be awful if you bought things, and then people gave you the same things."

"Really, I think you have bought enough, now," said the storekeeper. "Let's leave it. You can ride in the truck if you want to. You children ride in the back with the stove, and Mrs. Wood can sit with the driver."

"I want to sit with the driver, too," said Mike.

"All right," said the storekeeper. "Get in."

The two dogs were waiting outside the store. At last, all the things, children and dogs were in the truck. Everyone laughed as the truck went by.

They waved to the children. The children waved back. The dogs barked and barked.

Mike said, "How are you going to get that heavy stove into the room at the mine, Mister?"

The driver smiled. "I'll have plenty of help," he said. "You wait and see."

"I suppose you telephoned," said Mike.

"No, but the storekeeper did," said the driver. "We all have some secrets, don't we? Just look over there, right by the mine office!"

The truck slowly came to a stop. The children stared at the crowd, and then they all laughed and laughed.

CHAPTER 9

Quick Work

When the truck stopped at the mine office, a crowd of workmen stood waiting. The men were all smiling. Henry, Benny and Mike jumped out of the truck and helped Jessie and Violet out.

The driver helped Mrs. Wood down from the high seat. "We'll help you move these things into the building," said one man. "You tell us where you want them to go."

Mrs. Wood and the children and the driver went in. They looked around. The dogs ran around barking.

Just then Mr. Carter came out of the office.

"Oh, Mr. Carter, hello!" said Henry. "You are just the man we want."

"I want to see him too," said Mrs. Wood. "I want to ask him something."

"Ask away, my lady," said Mr. Carter with a smile.

"Well," said Mrs. Wood slowly, "I can hardly wait to make a pie. And I'd love to live right here in this room with my two boys."

"That's just what I said!" shouted Benny. "I said you've got to live somewhere, and why not here?"

"Yes, you did, Benny," agreed Mrs. Wood. "That is what gave me the idea. You see, Mr. Carter, the boys say there are watchmen up here all night. They would help me if I needed anything. And it wouldn't take long to put up some rough boards and make two rooms, would it? It would be so handy for me to start my pies early in the morning."

"Oh, what a wonderful idea!" cried Jessie. "We can help Mrs. Wood, too, Mr. Carter."

"Yes, I think it could be done," said Mr. Carter.

"I have talked with Mr. Gardner, the big boss, Mrs. Wood. He says if I say O.K., he says O.K."

"Oh, isn't this fun!" shouted Benny. "Who would put up the rough boards?"

Mr. Carter laughed. He pointed at the workmen who were bringing in the stove.

"Would they?" asked Violet softly.

"Yes, they would," said a workman who heard what Violet had said. "We have time off today."

"Then you could make the rooms today!" shouted Mike. He never liked to wait for anything.

A workman laughed at Mike. "You'll have to help us, son," he said.

"Oh, yes, I will," said Mike. "I'll be the one to tell you where the things go."

"That is called a boss," said the man. "Boss Mike."

Benny said, "Mike would be a good boss. He really would. And so would I. You see, that window will make Mike's room, and the next window will be Mrs. Wood's room. Every room will have one window so that it will have plenty of light."

"Not so bad!" said the man. "There is water in the office already. So we will just get longer pipes to go to your sink."

What a noise there was! Men were cutting holes in the floor for the pipes. Others were pounding away at the pipes. The dogs barked and barked. Mr. Carter telephoned three times and soon some long boards arrived at the door. More men came.

"My room can be small," said Mrs. Wood. "Just big enough for a bed."

"Mine ought to be bigger," said Mike. "Because Pat and I will have two beds, and I want another bed for Ben. I want him to sleep up here sometimes."

"That will be easy," said a man. "One small room, and one big one. Are you going to sleep here tonight?"

"No," said Mike. "No beds."

"What did you say?" shouted Benny. "Look out of the window!"

Another truck had just come. A bed was sticking out of the back. It was an Army cot.

Mr. Carter ran down the steps and said a few words to the driver.

Violet thought the driver said, "I'll be back soon," but she was not sure. The driver saw the children. He called, "Come on, kids! Help me take out these things."

The boys were delighted to help. They found some folding chairs under the cot.

"Where did these things come from?" asked Henry.

"From the neighbors," said the driver. "Everyone wants to help Mrs. Wood. These came from the store, but—." He stopped and said, "Don't ask me any more questions."

But Benny went right on. "What are those barrels for?"

"Two barrels of flour," said the driver.

"For pies," said Violet.

"Oh, barrels are very useful," said Benny. "Just put a board across two barrels and it makes a seat."

"It makes a table, too," said Jessie. "Remember our table in the barn on Surprise Island?"

Soon the children sat in a row on the long board. They were all watching the rooms go up.

"This is like a ball-game," said Henry.

"It's like a race," said Benny.

Henry said, "Some day we ought to have a race. We ought to have a fair race for Watch and Spot."

"Do you think so?" asked Mike. "Watch is a very fast runner."

"Oh, ho!" cried Benny. "You're afraid Watch will beat again!"

"No, I am not!" cried Mike. "Spotty is a fast runner, too."

"Now, boys, no fights!" said Henry. "Just enjoy yourselves. Who's coming now? It's a woman in a car."

"My neighbor from the blue house!" cried Mrs. Wood. She went to the door.

"Mike, come help Mrs. Smith with that box."

Mrs. Smith came in smiling. She shook hands with everyone. Then she said, "Mrs. Wood, all your friends want to help. They have looked over the things they can spare and everyone is giving you something. It's a Surprise Party."

"How kind you are!" said Mrs. Wood with tears in her eyes.

"We planned to have it next week, but Mr. Carter telephoned that now is the time. So everyone is coming today."

"Well, Mr. Carter is right," said Mrs. Wood. "This is the time I need it most."

"There are two sheets and two blankets in that box," said Mrs. Smith. "And more are on the way."

Another car came while she was talking. Then another and another. Soon the room was full of women with baskets and boxes. They brought everything that Mrs. Wood needed.

"Oh, oh!" said Jessie. "Isn't this fun, Violet? Look how fast the men are making shelves!"

"I'll put my pink cup on the shelf," shouted Benny.

"Look out of the window!" shouted Mike. A man was helping someone out of a car. It was Aunt Jane with her bright blue eyes and pink cheeks. She had a newspaper in her hand. Lady walked beside her.

All the children rushed over to Aunt Jane. All but Mike. He just stood and looked at the paper in her hand.

CHAPTER 10

Mike's Idea

"Oh, Aunt Jane," cried Jessie. "I'm so glad you came! Mrs. Wood is going to live here and make pies and sell them."

"Yes, I know," said Aunt Jane, laughing. "I know all about it. A little bird told me."

"Who told you?" asked Benny.

"Well, it was a big bird, after all," said Aunt Jane. "It was Mr. Gardner, the big boss. He sent a car for me."

Aunt Jane went into the big room.

Mike went up to her and held out his hand. She gave him the newspaper with a smile.

She said, "Maggie found it. I haven't had time to look at it, but I am sure it is the right one, Mike."

Then everyone tried to tell Aunt Jane about the two new rooms.

"They have doors!" said Benny. "Two doors, one in each room." The man who was putting up the doors laughed at Benny.

Jessie showed Aunt Jane the barrels of flour. Violet showed her the shelves. There were many dishes already on the shelves.

Aunt Jane had brought some things with her. A man came in with them. He had some big kettles and long spoons, and some small pans and small spoons.

"You have to get your own meals, Mrs. Wood," said Aunt Jane. "I thought the other cooking dishes would be too big for you."

"You are right, Miss Alden," said Mrs. Wood. "I must cook for my family, too. Where is Mike?"

Mike was not there.

"But where is he?" cried Jessie. "He was here just a minute ago."

"He's all right," said Mrs. Wood, laughing. "Mike can take care of himself pretty well. He must have some new idea."

Mike did have a new idea. He was in the office, talking to Mr. Carter. The newspaper was open on the desk, and they both were looking at the picture.

"See that man?" asked Mike. "He is the one Spotty growled at. He is wearing a hat, but you can't see if it is blue or not. Spotty must have seen him before."

"I have seen him before, too," said Mr. Carter, frowning.

"Where?" asked Mike.

"I don't know where," answered Mr. Carter.

"Well, he was at the fire," said Mike. "I saw him myself."

"And he has been at the mine," said Mr. Carter, "for here is his picture."

"I don't think he is a very good man," said Mike. "He looks rough to me."

"He looks rough to me, too," said Mr. Carter. "We must keep our eyes open, Mike."

There was a rap at the door.

"Come in," called Mr. Carter. It was Benny.

Benny said, "Oh, here you are, Mike! We lost you. I have another idea."

"Sit down," said Mr. Carter smiling. "We'll all sit down, and you tell us your idea."

"Well," began Benny, "you know Mike was making a new dog house for Spotty."

"No, I didn't know that," said Mr. Carter.

"Well, he was," said Benny. "And you know how Mike is. He isn't very neat."

"I am too, neat!" cried Mike.

"No, Mike. Listen! You had boards in the cellar. You had some boards by the heater, and some boards by the stairs, and some boards on both sides of the room."

"Well, yes, I did," said Mike. "But they were neat. They were standing up, neatly."

"But I mean they were on all sides of the cellar,"

cried Benny. "Don't you see? That's why the fire started on all sides of the house!"

"Good for you, Benny," said Mr. Carter. "The firemen think the fire was set by somebody."

"I didn't. I never did!" shouted Mike.

"Be quiet, Mike!" said Mr. Carter sharply. "I never said you did. I said somebody."

"Well, who?" asked Mike. "Who would set our house on fire with Spotty in the cellar?"

"I don't know yet," said Mr. Carter.

Then Benny said, "Think hard, Mike. What did you ever say to make anyone mad at you?"

"I never said anything."

"Yes, you must have," said Benny. "You know you talk a lot, Mike."

Mike began to think. "Maybe I did say something one day. But it was last summer," he said. "Maybe I said I was glad Miss Alden didn't sell her ranch to those three men. Remember that, Ben? Maybe I said I would know them in a minute if I saw them."

"Oh, my," said Mr. Carter.

Benny said, "But Mike, you wouldn't know them, because you never saw them!"

"I know it," said Mike. "I'm sorry now I said it. I suppose that man in the picture heard me, and he thought I knew him."

"Well, Mike," said Mr. Carter slowly, "you see that's why the story started that you set your own fire. The man in the picture may have heard you, and he was afraid of you. That would make him want to do something to hurt you the first chance he got."

"We can't prove it," said Benny.

"We will, though," said Mike. "You just wait."

"Yes, Mike, I think we will. Now, boys, I am going to tell you something. I know you both talk too much. But you must not talk too much about this."

"I won't," said Benny.

"I won't," said Mike.

"The three men who wanted to buy Miss Alden's ranch last summer are known to be bad men. When they found the uranium by accident, they did not tell anyone. They tried to buy the land for almost nothing. They were wanted in another state by the FBI. When they came to this state, the FBI caught them and put them in jail. But one of them is out now, I hear."

"Are you in the FBI?" asked Benny.

"I work for your grandfather, but I help the FBI too. I think this man may be one of those three, but you can't see his face clearly in the picture."

"They were mad because Aunt Jane wouldn't sell the ranch," said Benny.

"Right," said Mr. Carter. "He may do something to the mine if we don't stop him. So we are having two more night watchmen. Your mother will be perfectly safe up here."

"Let's go and help them settle things for the night," said Benny.

Things were going very well without them. Everyone was rushing around fixing the rooms. A real table was set up for the pies. One barrel of flour was opened. Pat came in with some more men. They were bringing big cans of cherries and peaches and blueberries and apples. They had great bags of sugar. There were piles of pie tins.

"Oh, how kind everyone is!" cried Mrs. Wood.

At last the oven worked, the refrigerator worked, and the sink worked. The cans of beautiful fruit were ready for pies. The rolling pins and boards were ready on the table.

Benny and Mike were in time to help set up the beds. Jessie and Violet began to put on the white sheets.

Then Mike surprised them all. He said, "Ma, I'd rather stay down at the house with Ben. You see, Miss Alden fixed up a nice room for me. She said I could bring all my things, and have Spotty in my room. I don't think it would be very nice for me to refuse it."

"Well, Mike!" cried Mr. Carter. "You certainly are getting to be a very nice, kind boy!"

"I'm very glad you are going to stay with us," said Aunt Jane with a smile.

"Yes, Mike," said his mother, "that was very thoughtful of you."

"I want to go with Ben," said Mike. "We can talk."

"Right! Right!" said Henry. "You can certainly talk!"

"I will take care of you, Ma," said Pat.

"Yes," said his mother smiling. "Pat will take care of me, and Mr. Carter says there are six night watchmen now instead of four. I wonder why?"

Mike and Benny looked at each other. They did not wonder at all.

CHAPTER 11

Pie Day

Everyone was tired that night. Even Mike and Benny did not talk very long. They put down a soft rug for Spotty, but he would not sleep on it. He lay down on the hard floor just under Mike's bed.

"That's just like a dog," said Mike. "They never stay where you put them."

"Lady always sleeps in Aunt Jane's room and Watch always sleeps in Jessie's room," said Benny. "He is really her dog, you know."

"No," said Mike, "I thought he was your dog."

"Well, he is all our dog," said Benny.

"I know what you mean, Ben," said Mike, yawning. He was too sleepy to argue.

"Good night," said Ben and went to his own room.

Both boys were soon asleep.

Up at the mine, Mrs. Wood and Pat went to sleep in their new beds. Mrs. Wood wanted to get up very early next morning.

It was about six o'clock when Mrs. Wood called Pat to a breakfast of eggs and bacon, toast and cereal and two glasses of milk. "I can hardly wait to begin a pie," she said to Pat. "You get washed at the sink and then come and eat. After that you can help me."

Pat said, "I bet Mike and Ben will be up here early, too. They don't want to miss anything, do they, Ma?"

"No. They don't miss very much," said Mrs. Wood with a smile.

Just as she finished washing the dishes, the other children came to the door.

"One of the men gave us a ride," said Benny. "See

what Violet has!" Violet had a piece of wood in her hands. There were big black letters on it. It was the new sign to go over the door.

Mrs. Wood read it. "MIKE'S MOTHER'S PLACE. Isn't that grand?"

Henry climbed up and nailed it over the door.

"Now tell us what to do, Mrs. Wood!" cried Jessie. She was excited. Her cheeks were very pink.

"Well, I have a good rule for pies," said Mrs. Wood. "You do not touch the crust with your hands. You put it between two pieces of wax paper before you roll it out. First you girls mix some flour with shortening in those big bowls. I'll show you."

"Jessie knows how," said Benny. "She is a fine pie maker."

"Yes, I am sure she is," said Mrs. Wood with a smile. "You boys turn on the ovens to 400. It's a wonderful stove you bought! Then set thirty of those tins in a row on the long table."

Soon everyone was hard at work. Mrs. Wood said, "I shall make only two kinds of pie the first day. We'll make cherry and apple. So you boys open the big cans, and leave them on the table. Just keep the dogs out of the way."

"I'll tie them up," said Mike.

"Oh, no," said Jessie. "Don't tie Watch. Listen, Watch, lie down!" Watch lay down at once and looked up at Jessie. He wagged his tail, but he did not get up.

"I wish Spotty could do that," said Mike. "I'll have to tie him."

"Some day we could teach him," said Benny. "But it will take a whole box of fig bars. When he starts to lie down, you give him a piece of a fig bar. When he gets up you say No! loud, like that."

"I'll make some fig cookies some day," said Mrs. Wood laughing.

They made thirty pies. The girls helped roll out the crust between two papers. They lifted the crust onto the tins without touching it.

"Oh, isn't this fun!" said Violet.

"You children seem to have fun just being kind to

somebody," said Mrs. Wood with a loving look at her.

"Somebody's coming!" shouted Mike from the open door. "It's a lady from town."

The lady laughed. She said, "I hear you sell pies."

"Yes," said Mike. "But they aren't done yet."

"When will they be done, little boy?" asked the lady.

"I'm not a little boy," answered Mike, "but I'll ask my mother."

"About ten o'clock," Mrs. Wood called out.

"About ten o'clock," repeated Mike.

"I'll be back then," said the lady. "I want an apple pie."

"We'll save one for you," said Mike. "I'll know you by your face. It's pretty."

"Well, thank you," said the lady, laughing. "Are you Mike?"

"Yes, I'm Mike, and it's my mother making pies."

When the pies were baked, they smelled delicious. They were nice and brown. The lady came back for her pie.

She said, "I told some people down on the street, and they are coming to buy pies."

"I hope there will be enough for the miners," said Mrs. Wood. "We really made the pies for the men."

"Let's make some more!" cried Jessie. "It will be too bad if the men don't get any."

The girls soon rolled out more pies. The boys opened another can of cherries. It was lucky they did so. When the whistle blew at noon, the men came pouring out of the mine. They saw the new sign, and they all wanted hot pies. Soon all the pies were sold.

"We haven't any left for us," said Mike sadly.

"Yes, Mike, I saved one pie," said his mother. "It was burned a little. I can cut it into seven pieces."

"I like pie burned a little," said Benny.

The family all sat around the long table to eat lunch. Maggie had sent up a large basket of sandwiches and salad and pink lemonade with ice in it. Everyone was very hungry.

"What do we do now?" asked Violet.

"We don't make any more pies, that's sure," said

Mrs. Wood. "We have done enough work for today."

"Let's have that race!" said Benny. "Let's race the dogs!"

"O.K." said Mike. "Let's race them down behind my old pink house. There is a big empty lot there. Plenty of room."

Jessie wanted to wash the dishes first. She filled the dish pan with hot soap suds. Then one by one, she slid the plates in, and washed them with a sponge. "I just love to do this," she said.

She rinsed them in hot water and set them in the drainer.

"We don't have to wipe them," she said. "They will dry themselves, because they are so hot."

In a very short time, the children were all in the back lot with the dogs. They had two enormous bones from the store.

Henry said, "Now Mike, you hold Spotty, and Jessie will hold Watch."

"Right on this line," said Benny.

"Yes," agreed Henry. "Then I will take one bone and go way down there by the fence. Ben, you take the other bone and come with me. Let the dogs smell the bones first."

The dogs wanted the bones very much. They tried to get away and follow Henry, but Jessie and Mike held them tight.

"You count, Violet," shouted Henry from the fence. "Say one, two, three, go, and then you let go of the dogs!"

When Henry and Benny reached the fence, they sat down on the ground with the bones. They held up the bones for the dogs to see.

"One, two, three, go!" shouted Violet. Away went the dogs. Watch went for Henry. Spotty went for Benny. They ran very fast. They were very even. Once Spotty got ahead. Then Watch got ahead. Then they were even again.

Suddenly Spotty seemed to turn. He slowed down. He skidded, like a car. Then he ran back, smelled around and began to dig.

"What's the matter?" cried Henry, puzzled.

"What's the matter with Spotty?" yelled Mike.

Spot went on digging. Then Watch stopped running. He trotted back to Spotty and began to dig, too.

Spotty began to growl. But he was not growling at Watch.

"Oh, isn't that strange?" said Jessie. The children came up and watched the dogs. The dirt flew everywhere. Spotty went on growling.

"Something must be buried here," said Henry. "Maybe a bone."

"It can't be a bone," said Mike. "Spotty wouldn't growl at a bone."

"Well, whatever it is, it is buried very deep," said Henry. "Just look at that hole."

Then Spotty began to growl and bark at the same time. He made a great noise. He put his white teeth into something, and sat back with it growling. It was a man's blue hat.

CHAPTER 12

An Empty Can

When Spot came up with the hat in his mouth, Benny cried, "The blue hat at last!"

"The man was afraid to wear it," shouted Mike.

"This proves that the man was up to no good," said Henry slowly.

"And he is the man in the picture!" shouted Mike again. "And this time I would know him for sure."

"I think he knows that," said Jessie. "We must tell Mr. Carter all about this."

"Well, Jessie, I'm sure Mr. Carter knows it already," said Benny.

Mike looked at Benny with a frown. The frown said, "Benny, don't talk too much."

Henry said, "Well, let's give the dogs the bones and go up and see Mr. Carter."

But they did not go. Watch suddenly began to dig again. Then the children noticed that the ground was soft. It did not take long. Watch did not growl, but soon he hit something hard. Henry leaned down and pulled out a big empty gasoline can.

"What do you know!" said Henry. "Lucky we found this. The man must have poured gasoline on the fire."

"Spotty must have seen him come into the cellar," said Mike. "That's why he didn't like him."

They all walked slowly to the mine office. They went in and told Mr. Carter all about the race.

"Which dog won the race?" asked Mr. Carter, laughing.

"Neither one," answered Mike. Then he told them about the dogs turning around to dig. He showed him the hat and the can.

"This is very, very important," cried Mr. Carter. "You have done very well. It won't be long now."

Then Benny suddenly opened his mouth. He looked at Mike and shut it again. Mike nodded, smiling.

When the two boys went out of the office, Benny whispered to Mike, "You remember Mr. McCarthy? The night watchman? He said he started to go to the fire that night."

"Yes," said Mike. "And he came right back, because he saw a man running, and his duty was right by the mine."

"That's right," said Benny. "You see what that means?"

"Oh, Ben," cried Mike. "I bet that man was going to blow up the mine! And he set the fire to get everybody to go to the fire!"

"Right!" said Benny. "I think we ought to tell Mr. Carter right away. It's neat!"

The boys went back alone. When they told this new story to Mr. Carter, he said, "Good for you, boys! It's a fine idea. I shall go right to work. I'll put two good men to work on it."

The boys were very pleased with themselves.

"We are working with the FBI, really, Ben," said Mike proudly.

"And I suppose the most important thing is not to talk," added Benny.

"I suppose so," said Mike sadly. "It's too bad we like to talk, Ben."

When the children came home to supper, Aunt Jane was delighted. She loved to hear them all talk. Maggie laughed and laughed at Mike and Benny, but they were careful what they said.

The children ate everything on the table. They ate hamburgers and rolls and tomatoes and beans and corn, and they drank many glasses of milk.

When everything was gone, Benny said, "Aunt Jane, did you know Mike could stand on his head?"

"No, I did not," said Aunt Jane.

"He can stand on his head forever," said Benny.

"Now, Benny, not forever," said Henry.

"But you never saw him," said Benny.

"I'll show you!" cried Mike. He put his head on the rug, and slowly lifted himself in the air.

"Good!" cried Aunt Jane. "That's wonderful, Mike."

Spotty went over to his young master, lay down and put his head on his paws. He shut his eyes.

"Spotty thinks you are going to stay there forever, Mike," said Jessie.

"I am," said Mike. His voice sounded funny, upside down.

"That's enough, old boy," said Henry. "Come on down!"

"Oh, no," cried Benny. "He can stand there forever, I tell you!"

"But I don't want him to stand there forever," said Aunt Jane. She could not help laughing. "It isn't good for you, Mike!"

"Why not?" asked Mike. "I don't mind."

"Yes," said Benny, nodding his head. "Mike can stay there all night, unless he goes to sleep."

"I could go to sleep standing on my head," said Mike, upside down.

"Oh, come on, Mike," said Henry. "Get up! You've been there long enough!"

But Mike did not move. "I'm very comfortable," he said. "You can all read a book. And I'll just stand on my head and rest."

At last Aunt Jane begged him to stop. "Please, Mike!" she said. "I believe you can stand there a long time."

"All night?" asked Mike. "Do you believe I could stand there all night?"

"Yes! Yes!" cried Aunt Jane. "Only do come down! It's a wonderful trick."

So Mike stood on his feet at last, and fixed his hair. "I could have stayed there a lot longer," he said.

Then Henry made Watch do his tricks. Watch sat up and begged. He "spoke." He was a "dead" dog. He shook hands with everybody. Then Maggie gave him a big bone.

The boys did tricks all the evening. They had only

two fights. Then Mike said suddenly, "Aunt Jane—" Then he stopped.

"Go on," said Aunt Jane.

"Well, I ought to say, Miss Alden," said Mike.

"No, you call me Aunt Jane. I wish you would."

So Mike went on. "Aunt Jane, you gave me that newspaper, you know."

"Yes, I did."

"Well, you said you didn't look at it. Will you look at it now?"

"Certainly I will, if you want me to," said the lady.

"It's just the picture," said Mike, taking it out of his pocket. "Just look at my brother, Pat, and remember I was right here, standing beside him. But the picture cut me off." Mike pointed. He gave the picture to Aunt Jane.

But Aunt Jane suddenly saw the picture of the short man. She frowned. Then she cried, "I know that man! He is one of the men who tried to buy my ranch. I'd know him anywhere!"

Henry was excited. "That was last summer. It was

the time you were alone in the house. We all went to the store, and the men came while we were away. Are you sure, Aunt Jane?"

"Of course I'm sure!" cried Aunt Jane. "I never liked those three men. I'd know them anywhere."

"Well, Mike, what do you think about that!" shouted Benny.

Just then the telephone rang. It was for Benny.

"Hello," said Benny.

"This is Mr. Carter," said the voice. "You can tell the rest about this. We found a lot of wires behind the mine. Someone was going to blow it up. Thanks to you and Mike, we got the wires out."

"Good!" said Benny. "And listen to this! Aunt Jane knows the man in the picture. He is the man that just got out of jail, I bet."

"What? What? I'll be right down," said Mr. Carter.

When he came down, he asked Aunt Jane many questions. At last he said, "We know the man, and we can prove it. I don't think it will be very long now. We just have to find him."

CHAPTER 13

The Party

Mr. Carter had said, "It won't be long now." But it was longer than he thought. Nobody saw the man. Benny and Mike were always watching, but they never saw him. There seemed to be no stranger in town.

The pie business was doing well. Every day Mrs. Wood and the girls made sixty pies. The boys sold them all.

"We are making money," said Jessie. "People are very good to us. And the insurance helped."

"Yes, my dear," said Mrs. Wood. "I think I can earn a good living this way."

"Yes," said Violet. "We have so much practice, we can make them faster and faster!"

"It was a very good idea," said Henry, "having Mike's Mother's Place. I never get tired of selling pies. The men are so glad to get them."

Mrs. Wood said, "When you go back to school, I can hire two girls to help me. I know two nice girls."

"Some day we ought to have a party," said Jessie. "The people have been so kind."

"A Pie Party!" cried Benny. "Give everybody a pie."

Mrs. Wood laughed. "Not a whole pie, Benny," she said. "We could give everybody a piece of pie, and some coffee."

"And milk," said Benny.

"Well, all right, milk," agreed Mrs. Wood.

"Have it Saturday night, when all the men could come," said Violet.

"Have it *this* Saturday night!" shouted Benny.

"We can ask Mr. Carter and Mr. Gardner," said Henry.

"And we can make pies all day," said Jessie, "and have the party in the evening."

Everyone thought this was a fine idea. When they told Mr. Gardner he laughed. He said, "Go ahead. I'll help you. It will surely be very lonesome here when you four Aldens go back to school in the Fall."

Mrs. Wood and Jessie and Violet wore white. They made white caps.

They made white caps for the boys, too. They made big white aprons. The boys got a printing set and printed MIKE'S MOTHER'S PLACE on the front of their big aprons. They had many cans of milk and hot coffee.

Then the people began to come to the party. The two dogs ran around having a wonderful time. They loved everybody, and they were good dogs.

There were plenty of chairs, because Mr. Carter had sent them. He sent movies too.

He said, "I have some beautiful pictures of the

MIKE'S MOTHER'S PLACE
MIKE'S MOTHER'S PLACE
MIKE'S MOTHER'S PL

South Seas. The people will like to see the banana trees and the monkeys."

When it was dark, the movies began. The people sat in rows and watched the show. They clapped and laughed at the monkeys. Watch had a chair between Jessie and Benny. He watched the picture with the rest. Next came Mike and then Spot. Mr. Carter sat on the end near the door. All the windows were open and the door was open. Benny whispered to Mike, "This would be a good time for somebody to blow up the mine."

"No, the watchmen are there," Mike whispered.

Mike put his arm around Spotty's neck. Everyone looked at the picture except Mike. He never knew why he looked out the door, but he did and Spotty looked too. He saw a man walking slowly by. Then suddenly he felt the hair on Spotty's neck move. Spotty looked at the door and growled.

Mr. Carter heard Spotty growl. He jumped up, and dashed out of the door. Mike and Spotty dashed after him.

They all saw a man running in the darkness. But Spotty could run faster than the man. Soon he caught the man's leg. He held him, growling, until Mr. Carter came. Mike never knew how strong Mr. Carter's hands were.

The watchmen ran up and soon the man was taken away.

"The man in the blue hat!" cried Mike.

"Yes, Mike, I think it is," said Mr. Carter. "Spotty knew him."

"Spotty ran faster than he did in the race," said Mike.

"I guess he did," said Mr. Carter. "Now, Mike, don't say a word. Just go back quietly."

"Can't I tell Ben?" asked Mike.

"Yes, if you whisper. Don't let anyone else know about this. It will spoil the party."

CHAPTER 14

Ben or Mike?

When Mike and Spotty went back, Mike whispered, "Ben, we just caught the man in the blue hat."

"You did?" said Benny. "Did he have on a blue hat?"

"He didn't have on any hat at all," said Mike. "I told you he wouldn't."

"I wish you had told me before," said Benny. "Watch and I would have come, too."

"I had no time," said Mike. "Sh-h-h, don't say a word!"

Then the show was over. The lights went on. Everyone sat around eating pie and drinking coffee. Mr. Carter came back very quietly.

The boys looked at him but they did not say a word.

"It's all over," Mr. Carter whispered to Mike and Benny.

"Where is that man?" asked Mike.

"Well, he is in jail again. This time he will stay there," said Mr. Carter. "That man was wanted in four states! You boys helped me a great deal. And best of all, you did not talk."

"Wait till I tell Henry!" cried Benny. "He thinks I can't stop talking."

"I'll tell him myself," smiled Mr. Carter. "And Jessie will like to know, too. She's a mother to you, Benny."

"Yes, I know," said Benny.

"She always keeps care of you, Ben," said Mike.

"*Takes* care of me," said Benny.

"Well, *takes* care, then," agreed Mike. He didn't

even start to argue. Benny was quite surprised.

With everyone gone, the Woods, the Aldens and Mr. Carter were left alone in the big room.

Mr. Carter said, "Please sit down, all of you. I want to tell you something."

When they were quiet, he said, "The hunt for the man in the blue hat is over. The man has been caught, and the mystery is solved."

"Oh, how?" asked Aunt Jane in excitement.

Then Mr. Carter told her about the man. He told her about Spotty growling.

"You don't need to growl any more, Spotty," said Mr. Carter. He patted the dog's smooth head. "The man has gone away."

"Well, I am glad," said Violet softly. "I know it was exciting for the boys, but I didn't like it at all."

"No," said Mr. Carter, looking at Violet with a smile, "neither did I."

"Well," said Mike, "now it's all over, it was my mystery, wasn't it?"

"Oh, no, it wasn't!" cried Benny. "It was mine!"

"My dog found the blue hat!" shouted Mike.

"But my dog helped him. And Watch found the tin can!" said Benny.

Then Mike suddenly stopped. He said, "Yes, Ben, I think it was your mystery after all. Because it was your mine."

"Well," said Benny slowly, "maybe it was yours, because it was your house that burned up."

"Well, well!" said Henry, smiling at Mike. "How you have changed, Mike!"

"That's what I say," said Mrs. Wood. "Mike is getting to be a very nice, thoughtful boy. He doesn't argue so much. I said it did him good to play with Benny."

Henry laughed. "And you remember I said it was good for Benny to play with Mike! They are quite a pair."

"Yes, boys, you are quite a pair," said Mr. Carter. His eyes began to twinkle. "Let me give you something to think about. Maybe you two boys will be together next summer, too. But not here."

"Where," cried Jessie, "will we all be together?"

"Well, you children will all be together, but the rest is a secret."

"Oh, a secret? Grandfather's secret, I suppose," said Henry. "He is always a little ahead of us."

"Yes, I can tell you that much. You children and Mike, and your grandfather are included in the secret."

"And Spotty and Watch?" asked Mike.

"Yes, Watch, but not Spotty."

The children were thinking hard. They had no idea what it was all about.

Jessie asked the last question. "Will you be there, too, Mr. Carter?"

"No," said Mr. Carter. He looked at Jessie with a funny little smile. "And I shall certainly be very sorry for myself."

After that, Mr. Carter shook his head at every question. He would not tell another thing.

Then Mike said, "I'm not going to ask Mr. Carter any more. He don't want to tell us. I mean *doesn't.*"

"Well, well, you're learning, Mike," said Henry. "Maybe you'll be a schoolteacher yet."

"Oh, no, I won't. I'm going to be an FBI man," said Mike.

"Yes, and he may," said Mr. Carter. "He and Benny talk all the time. But I want you all to know that they know when to keep still."

Benny was thinking. Then he went over to Mr. Carter and put his hand on Mr. Carter's shoulder. "I think this really was Mike's mystery," he said. "It was his dog that found the hat. And he would have found it if I had stayed home with Grandfather, and never come out here at all."

"Good for you, Benny," said everyone.

"What a kind boy you are, Benny," said Mrs. Wood.

"That was good of you, Ben," said Mike. "Thank you."

Mike was so polite that everyone laughed. But it was Mike's mystery forever and ever.